The Adventures of Sip & Tip

by Airica Savage Clapper

illustrated by Kristina Tartara

"Little Waves organization educates children about environmental concerns and provides opportunities for children to take care of our earth."

ISBN 978-0-578-69908-0

www.littlewaves.org
Edited by Krista Hill, L Talbott Editorial Services
The images were created digitally using Procreate.

To the children of our earth - She is in your hands. Take good care of her.
- Airica

To my girls - May you always find your way to doing something greater.
- Kristina

Sip the straw stood proudly in his container, watching customers stream into the coffee shop.

"Hey, Tip!" he shouted to his best buddy, Tip the water bottle, who was chilling in the cooler. "Maybe today! Maybe today is the day someone will pick us!"

Being a straw and a water bottle was only the beginning. Once they served their purpose, they could be taken to the Recycling Center. There, they could be changed into something else - something new!

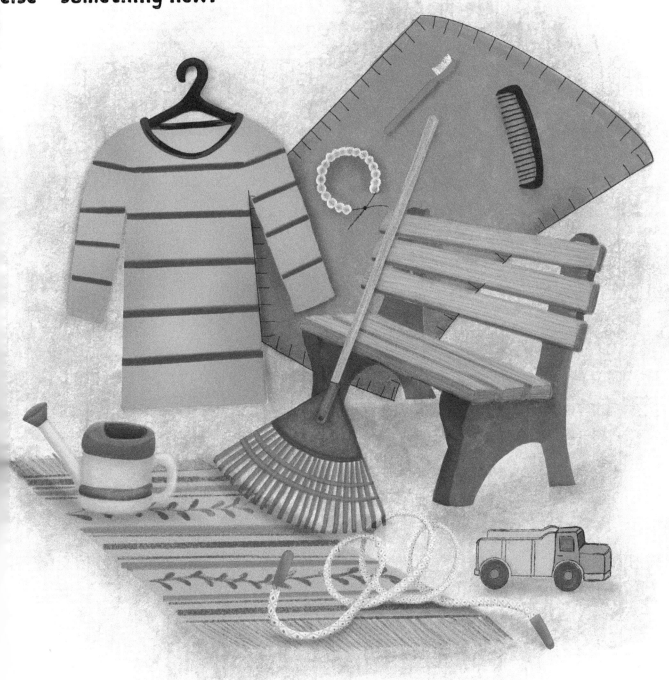

Being recycled was every plastic's dream!

A little girl came into the shop, followed by her mother. Sip heard the magic words, "Iced tea, please!" He could hardly contain himself!

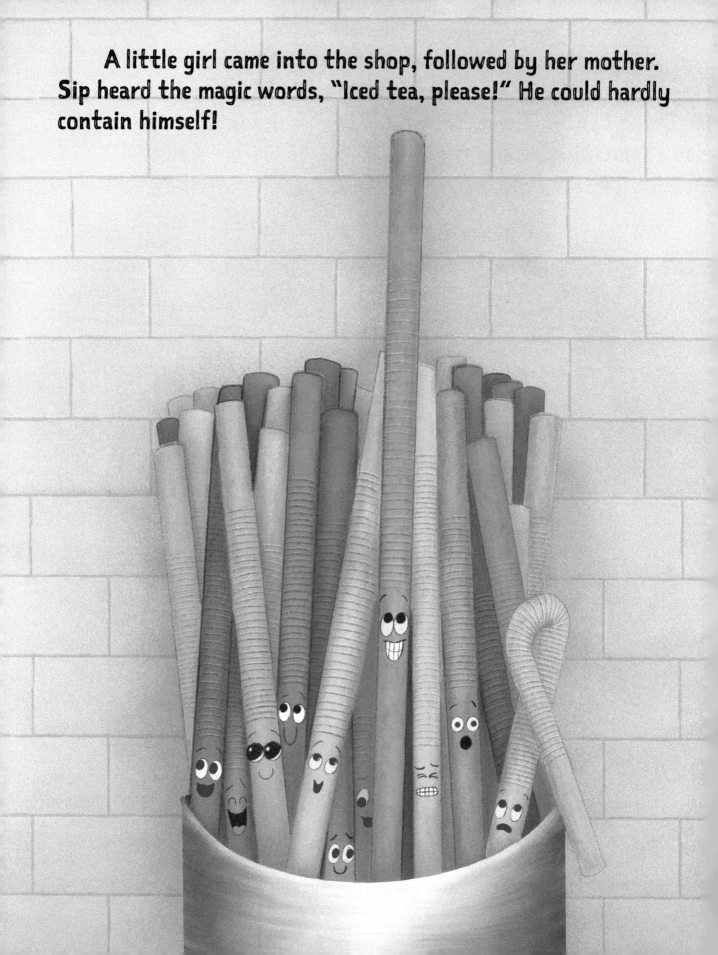

The girl scooped up Tip from the cooler, and Tip bubbled with excitement as her mother then lifted Sip from his container and plopped him into her iced tea!

"Can you believe our luck?" he said. The two friends beamed as they were carried out of the coffee shop together.

Seagulls squawked overhead and waves crashed. The bright sun warmed the sand.

"Where are we?" Tip asked.
"I don't know," replied Sip, "but it sure is pretty!"
"I like this place," Tip said.
Sip grinned. "Me too."

The little girl and her mother enjoyed their day. They built sandcastles, splashed in the water, and searched for shells.

Later, the two packed up and placed **Sip** and **Tip** in a recycling bin. Throughout the day, many people had visited the beach. The garbage cans and recycling bins were overflowing.

Suddenly, a gust of wind caught Sip and Tip and swept them into the air. They tumbled to the ground! Covered in sand, the two plastics baked in the hot sun.

"What's going to happen to us, Sip?" Tip whispered.
Sip frowned. "I don't know," he replied.
The two dozed off as the sky turned dark and the stars appeared, one by one.

Early the next morning, Sip and Tip awoke to a scary sight! Huge, white puffy things stood over them. They waddled around, their heads bobbing up and down.

OH NO!

Two crazy birds began to toss Sip and Tip into the air. They crunched them in their beaks and shook them wildly.

"Get em, Squawk!" said one.

"Here, Screech! Catch!" said the other.

Finally, Screech and Squawk flew out over the water and dropped Sip and Tip. The two plastics bobbed helplessly in the waves.

Sip heard a great splash behind him. A mighty giant surfaced. It chomped down on Sip so tightly he couldn't escape.

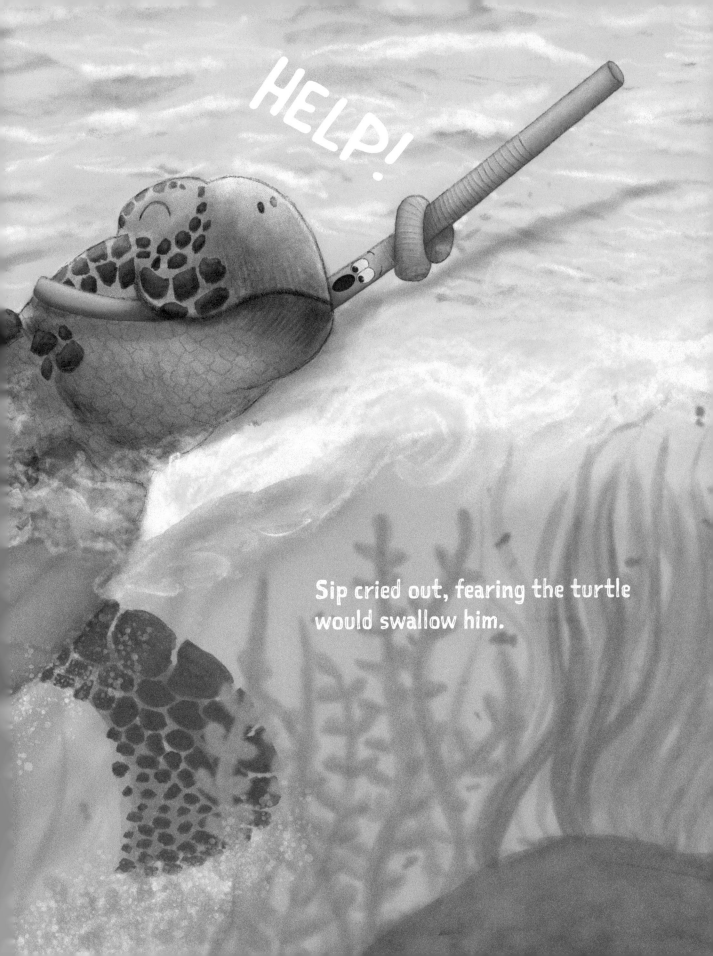

Suddenly, a huge wave came crashing down, knocking Sip from the turtle's mouth. Sip tumbled and tumbled until he was washed back onto the beach.

"Whew! That was close!" Sip exclaimed.
"It sure was!" a voice behind him said.

Sip whirled around. "Tip! I thought I lost you forever!"
Tip grinned. "I'm fine!" he replied, brushing seaweed out of his face.

Along came two boys collecting plastics from the beach. As they drew near, Sip said, "I hope they'll rescue us. I'm starting to get sunburned!"

"And I am thirsty!" Tip declared.

One boy picked up Sip and the other reached for Tip.

Soon, the two plastics found themselves back in the recycling bin.

Later that day, Sip and Tip were startled by a loud, roaring sound. They were lifted into the air and dropped into a large pile of other items being recycled. Things began to rumble and shake. "What's happening?" Sip cried.

A dirty old bait container emerged from under a crumpled piece of tin foil.

"Don't be afraid," he said. "We are on our way to the Recycling Center!"

"Hooray!" Sip shouted.

They arrived at the Recycling Center. After being sorted, they went through a special machine.

Sip and Tip became part of a brand-new swing set. The duo ended up back on the very beach where their adventure had started. They were as happy as the children who played on them from sunup to sundown.

Sip sighed. "Maybe some of our friends from the coffee shop will join us here someday. This is a great place!"

Splat! A big ball of white goo landed on Tip's swing. He looked up to see Screech and Squawk perched on top of the swing set.

Tip frowned. "Yes, it is a great place! *Most* of the time!"

Join the Little Waves Rescue Team!

Sip and Tip would love your help! There are many ways YOU can make a difference. Like the seagulls and turtle in our story, many animals encounter plastics and other hazards in their homes. These items are unsafe and harmful to our earth, our wild animals, and to us. Small efforts can make a BIG difference. Here are a few things YOU can do today:

- Use a reusable water bottle.

- Help rinse and sort recycling items at home.

- Reuse and repurpose toys, clothes, and other household items by hosting a neighborhood trade.

- Skip the straw and kid's cup at your next restaurant visit. Ask for a regular glass without a straw or bring your favorite kid's cup from home.

- Support restaurants and companies that are earth-friendly or make products from recycled items.

- Buy snacks in bulk rather than single-use and place them in reusable snack-sized containers.

- Plant a garden or a tree each year.

- Pack litterless lunches - use parchment paper or reusable food storage bags.

- Bring reusable shopping bags anywhere you might make a purchase.

- Take a visit to your local recycling center to understand the guidelines in your community.

- Host or join a beach clean-up or community clean-up in your area.

- Write letters or draw pictures and send them to your state leaders asking them to protect our waterways and earth.

- If you see it, retrieve it! On your next outing, take a reusable bag to collect items that belong in the trash or recycling bin. You can also get your own Little Waves Rescue Bag by visiting our website. Remember, straws need to be placed in a larger plastic container in order to be properly recycled. Always have an adult help you.

For more information on ways you can help our earth or get involved with the Little Waves Organization, please visit www.littlewaves.org and follow @makinglittlewaves on Instagram.

CPSIA information can be obtained
at www.ICGtesting.com
Printed in the USA
BVHW020714150820
586010BV00006B/5